MiSTER BUD

WEARS THE CONE

CARTER GOODRICH

SIMON & SCHUSTER BOOKS FOR YOUNG READERS
NEW YORK   LONDON   TORONTO   SYDNEY   NEW DELHI

For Anne and Joe, with love

SIMON & SCHUSTER BOOKS FOR YOUNG READERS * An imprint of Simon & Schuster Children's Publishing Division * 1230 Avenue of the Americas, New York, New York 10020 * Copyright © 2014 by Carter Goodrich * All rights reserved, including the right of reproduction in whole or in part in any form. * SIMON & SCHUSTER BOOKS FOR YOUNG READERS is a trademark of Simon & Schuster, Inc. * For information about special discounts for bulk purchases, please contact Simon & Schuster Special Sales at 1-866-506-1949 or business@simonandschuster.com. * The Simon & Schuster Speakers Bureau can bring authors to your live event. For more information or to book an event, contact the Simon & Schuster Speakers Bureau at 1-866-248-3049 or visit our website at www.simonspeakers.com. * Design by Dan Potash * The text for this book is set in Gorey. * The illustrations for this book are rendered in watercolor. * Manufactured in China * 0314 SCP * 10 9 8 7 6 5 4 3 2 1 * Library of Congress Cataloging-in-Publication Data * Goodrich, Carter, author, illustrator. * Mister Bud wears the cone / Carter Goodrich. — First edition * pages cm * Summary: "Mister Bud and Zorro have learned how to get along. They made it through Zorro's outfit. But now Mister Bud has to wear … the cone." Provided by publisher. * ISBN 978-1-4424-8088-9 (hardcover : alk. paper) — ISBN 978-1-4424-8089-6 (eBook) * [1. Dogs—Fiction.] I. Title. PZ7.G61447Mi 2013 * [E]—dc23 * 2012040030

MISTER BUD HAD A BAD HOT SPOT.
HE CHEWED AND LICKED IT ALL NIGHT.

IN THE MORNING IT WAS WORSE.

"Sorry, guy. It's no fun. I know."

MISTER BUD WAS GETTING ALL THE ATTENTION.

AND THE SCHEDULE WAS ALL MESSED UP.

"Here you go. Just while I'm gone."

IT WAS TIME FOR THE CONE.
MISTER BUD HATED THE CONE.

HE TRIED TO GET IT OFF,
BUT IT WOULDN'T BUDGE.

THEN ZORRO TRIED . . . BUT IT WAS STUCK TIGHT.

AFTER A WHILE, ZORRO LOST INTEREST. . . .

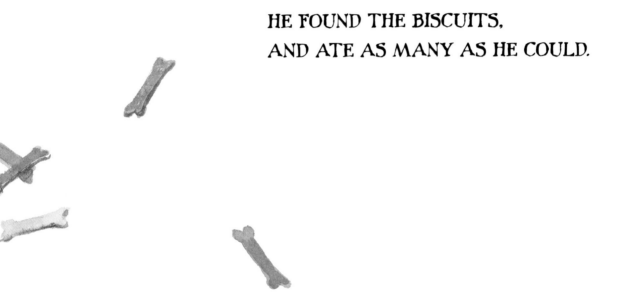

HE FOUND THE BISCUITS,
AND ATE AS MANY AS HE COULD.

BUT MISTER BUD COULDN'T REACH THEM.

AND WHEN HE TRIED TO DRINK, HE SPILLED HIS WATER DISH.

WHEN THEY PLAYED, THE CONE
MADE IT HARD FOR MISTER BUD TO SEE.

ZORRO THOUGHT IT WAS FUNNY AND TEASED MISTER BUD.

THEN HE GOT INTO MISTER BUD'S TOYS. . . .

BUT WHEN MISTER BUD TRIED TO GET HIS MOUSE BACK . . .

THE CONE KNOCKED SOMETHING OVER.

AND IT BROKE.

NOW YOU DID IT!

MISTER BUD FELT SO BAD, HE DIDN'T JOIN ZORRO FOR WAIT AND WATCH TIME . . .

. . . OR FOR GREET AND MAKE A FUSS TIME.

"Uh-oh."

BUT MISTER BUD DIDN'T GET IN TROUBLE AFTER ALL.

"Poor guy. It's hard to see with this thing on, isn't it?"

IN FACT . . .

MISTER BUD GOT HIS OWN SPECIAL TREAT.

BUT HE SHARED IT WITH ZORRO ANYWAY.

EVERYTHING WAS BACK TO NORMAL.

AND THAT WAS THE END OF THE CONE.

FOR NOW. . . .